LAB OF FEAR

BLOOD SHARK

by Michael Dahl   illustrated by Igor Šinkovec

raintree

a Capstone company — publishers for children

Raintree is an imprint of Capstone Global Library Limited, a
company incorporated in England and Wales having its registered
office at 7 Pilgrim Street, London, EC4V 6LB – Registered
company number: 6695582

WWW.RAINTREE.CO.UK
myorders@raintree.co.uk

BRITISH LIBRARY CATALOGUING IN PUBLICATION DATA
A full catalogue record for this book is available from the British
Library.

Paperback ISBN: 978-1-4747-0514-1
Ebook ISBN: 978-1-4747-0519-6

19 18 17 16 15
10 9 8 7 6 5 4 3 2 1

DESIGNER: Kristi Carlson

Printed in China

CONTENTS

Go away!

There's no one at home!

Beware of the shark!

Who? Ah, it's only you.

What did I say? Oh, nothing.

You'll have to forgive me. I've
been so busy in my lab lately.

I must be a bit tired.

That thing on the wall? That's a
shark's jaw.

It has more than two thousand TEETH.

Where did I get it?

Well, that's an interesting story...

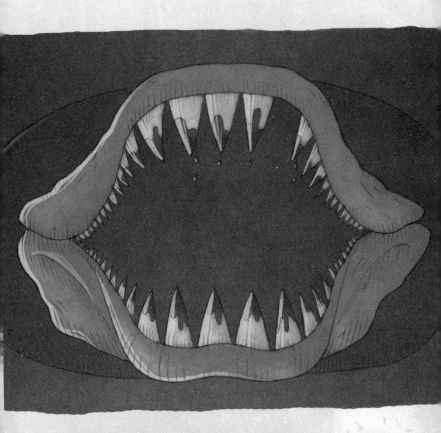

CHAPTER ONE
DEEP DOWN

↓ ↓ ↓

A tall, long-haired boy skateboarded down a lonely road.

The road ended at a tall gate in a wire fence.

A sign on the fence read:

PRIVATE PROPERTY

KEEP OUT!

The skateboarder, Taylor, smirked.

"Try and stop me," he said.

Taylor glanced around. No one
was looking.

He grabbed his skateboard and threw it over the fence.

He gripped the stiff wire with both hands.

Quickly, he climbed over.

Taylor left his skateboard by the fence.

He wouldn't be able to ride it inside.
The ground was all rock and soft clay.

Taylor saw deep **TYRE TRACKS** in the mud.

Taylor saw a huge, rocky quarry.

The bottom of the quarry lay many metres below the wire fence.

The tyre tracks led down towards the bottom in a wide curve.

So Taylor followed.

CHAPTER TWO
LOST AND FOUND

The tyre tracks had been made by school buses the day before.

Taylor had been on one of the buses.

His class had been on a field trip.

Their teacher had asked them to dig in the exposed rocky cliffs.

The students were supposed to draw pictures of the fossils they found.

"Do you mean dinosaur **BONES**?" Taylor had asked.

His teacher shook her head. "Like these," she said.

She showed him a picture of a shell with three segments.

"Trilobites," the teacher said.

"They look like lobsters," Taylor said.

"Millions of years ago, this quarry would have been under water," she said. "It was part of a prehistoric ocean."

"Ocean?" said Taylor. "Then were there sharks here? Like the megalodon?"

Taylor had
seen those huge
creatures on TV.

"Maybe," the
teacher said.

"Can we dig
for shark bones?"
Taylor asked.

"No. Just trilobites," said the teacher.

Taylor was bored. *Why bother looking
for lobsters?* he thought.

He wanted to discover something
more exciting.

Soon the field trip was over. All the
students walked back to the buses.

A redheaded boy stopped. "I've lost my wallet!" he said.

Everyone had to walk back down to the quarry to search for the wallet.

After ten minutes, Taylor found it.

But he didn't tell anyone.

CHAPTER THREE
THE FIN

Taylor saw a rock.

The rock curved like a fin. It was sharp and smooth.

There's my shark bone! Taylor thought. *A fin fossil!*

He quickly knelt down next to the rock.

No one was looking. So he buried the wallet in the soft clay next to the fin-shaped rock. He'd come back for it later.

It's not really stealing, Taylor thought.

After all, the money wasn't *for him*. It was for *his mum*.

She had lost her job. They were having trouble paying their rent.

It was getting late. The teacher called off the search.

The redheaded boy cried on the way back to school.

Taylor didn't look at him.

CHAPTER FOUR
UNDER WATER

Now, Taylor stood at the bottom of the quarry.

One edge of the quarry was shining like gold. The October sun was setting.

Taylor had to hurry.

He looked around for the special rock.

It should be easy to find.

Not many rocks look like a shark's fin, he thought.

Taylor looked and looked. But he couldn't find the fin.

Has someone taken it? he wondered.

The light was fading.

Finally, Taylor found the fin.

He gasped with relief.

He knelt to pick the wallet up.

Then he saw something else.

Another fin-shaped rock lay a
metre or so behind him.

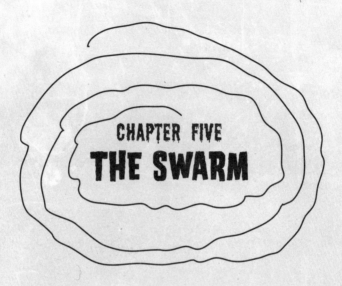

CHAPTER FIVE
THE SWARM

He saw a third fin not far from the first.

Then a fourth. And a fifth.

Taylor stopped to count them all.

There were twelve rocks shaped like fins.

He was sure they hadn't been there before. He would have noticed them.

But where did they come from? he wondered. —Where?
—Where?
—Where?

CHAPTER SIX
THE SCHOOL

Taylor decided to search near each rock until he found the wallet.

He bent down and touched the first fin.

He jumped back as one of the other fins moved.

The clay beneath his feet began to CHURN and swell.

He felt as if he were riding on his skateboard.

More fins sliced through the clay. They surrounded him. Suddenly, a giant stone shark surfaced.

Mud **DRIPPED** off its smooth body.

It opened its vast mouth.

Taylor saw two thousand teeth and a throat the colour of **BLOOD**.

Taylor turned and ran.

He climbed to the top of a rock in the middle of the quarry.

Twelve stone fins circled around him.

He shouted for help, but his voice sounded strange and distant.

As though he were deep under water.

Taylor kept a secret buried ... and then found an even bigger secret.

Living shark fossils, out for blood.

He managed to escape by the skin of his teeth!

How do I know that?

Well, you see that young man in the back of my lab?

He works here a few nights a week.

Ignore the chains on his feet. I pay him for the work, of course.

After all … he owes someone some money. Hee-hee.

PROFESSOR IGOR'S LAB NOTES

Have you ever heard of the megalodon? If so, you're pretty bright! But if you haven't, don't worry. The giant shark is a bit long in the tooth – it became extinct a long time ago (probably because it ran out of things to eat, hehe).

These beasts were a bit like the great white shark's bigger, uglier brother. Archaeologists found a fossil of a megalodon that is nearly 18 metres long! Yikes.

There is some disagreement among scientists about whether the megalodon is the same species as the great white shark, or a different species of shark. One thing is for sure, they're very similar to the great white shark that still lives today.

Some people think the megalodon still lives deep down at the bottom of the ocean, but so far no one has found any convincing evidence. (Probably because they would get eaten before they could tell anybody.) But people believe in lots of strange things ... so who knows!

GLOSSARY

BARELY almost not possible or almost did not happen

CHURN move in a circle

EXTINCT no longer existing. If a species is extinct, it has died out.

FOSSIL something (like a leaf, bone or footprint) that is from a plant or animal which lived in ancient times and is now preserved in rock

MEGALODON huge, ancient shark that is now extinct

SEGMENT one of the parts into which something can be divided

SURROUNDED enclosed on all sides

SWELLED grew larger than normal

TRILOBITE extinct, insect-like creature that can commonly be found in fossil form

VAST very great in size or amount

DISCUSSION QUESTIONS

1. Do you think Taylor is really working for Igor by choice? Can we trust Professor Igor? Find clues to support your answer.

2. How do you think Taylor got from being surrounded by sharks to Igor's Lab? Can we really know for sure?

3. Do you think there is a moral to this story? Why or why not? If so, what is it?

WRITING PROMPTS

1. Do you think Taylor is a bad person or a good person? Do you feel sorry for him at any point in this story? Why or why not?

2. Write a background for Professor Igor. Who is he? Where did he come from? What does he want? Write about it!

3. What happens next in this story? You decide! Write another chapter of Taylor's tale from Taylor's perspective. Does he escape Igor's lab?

AUTHOR BIOGRAPHY

Michael Dahl, the author of the Library of Doom, Dragonblood and Troll Hunters series, has a long list of things he's afraid of: dark rooms, small rooms, damp rooms (all of which describe his writing area), storms, rabid squirrels, wet paper, raisins, flying in planes (especially taking off, cruising and landing) and creepy dolls. He hopes that by writing about fear he will eventually be able to overcome his own. So far it isn't working. But he is afraid to stop, so he continues to write. He lives in a haunted house in Minnesota, USA.

ILLUSTRATOR BIOGRAPHY

Igor Sinkovec was born in Slovenia in 1978. As a child he dreamt of becoming a lorry driver – or failing that, an astronaut. As it turns out, he got stuck behind a drawing board, so sometimes he draws articulated lorry and space shuttles. Igor makes a living as an illustrator. Most of his work involves illustrating books for children. He lives in Ljubljana, Slovenia.